This book belongs to:

Backis

Published in 1990 by
Stewart, Tabori & Chang, Inc.
575 Broadway, New York, New York 10012

Translated from the French by Jane R. Becker

Library of Congress Cataloging-in-Publication Data

Billiet, Daniel.
    [Grande invasion des Mange-Pierre. English]
    The great invasion of the stone moles / Daniel Billiet. Nicole
Rutten.
        p.   cm.
    Translation of: Le grande invasion des Mange-Pierre.
    Summary: Chaos overtakes a small town overrun with strange stone-
eating moles, until one girl convinces the townspeople to
understand and appreciate the creatures.
    ISBN 1-55670-153-5
    [1. Moles (Animals)—Fiction.]   I. Rutten, Nicole.   II. Title.
PZ7.B495Gr   1990
[E]—dc20   89-26371
                                                    CIP
                                                    AC

Distributed in the U.S. by Workman Publishing,
708 Broadway, New York, New York 10003
Distributed in Canada by Canadian Manda Group,
P.O. Box 920 Station U, Toronto, Ontario M8Z 5P9
Distributed in all other territories by
Little, Brown and Company, International Division,
34 Beacon Street, Boston, Massachusetts 02108

Printed in Belgium

10 9 8 7 6 5 4 3 2 1

The Great Invasion of the Stone Moles

Daniel Billiet ■ Nicole Rutten

Stewart, Tabori & Chang
New York

It all started one beautiful summer evening.
The cathedral clock had just chimed nine,
when something happened that turned our little town
upside down and changed my life.

We were quietly enjoying a drink at a sidewalk café, when
suddenly, a woman leapt up, screaming in terror.
The pigeons took to the sky, and the dogs began to growl.
    "Look . . ." gasped the screaming woman, "there, there!"
And there, in the spot where she was pointing, we saw the ground move.
The pavement rose, making a small hill from which emerged
first a pointed nose and then two large, clawed paws.
It was a mole! A white mole. A white mole eating the stone!

The screaming woman fainted.
The townspeople fled, knocking over chairs and tables,
jostling each other, and running off in all directions.
It was chaos!
Terrified, the stone-eating mole tried to escape.
A few brave townspeople ran after him,
but just as two large hands were about to grab him,
he disappeared into the ground.

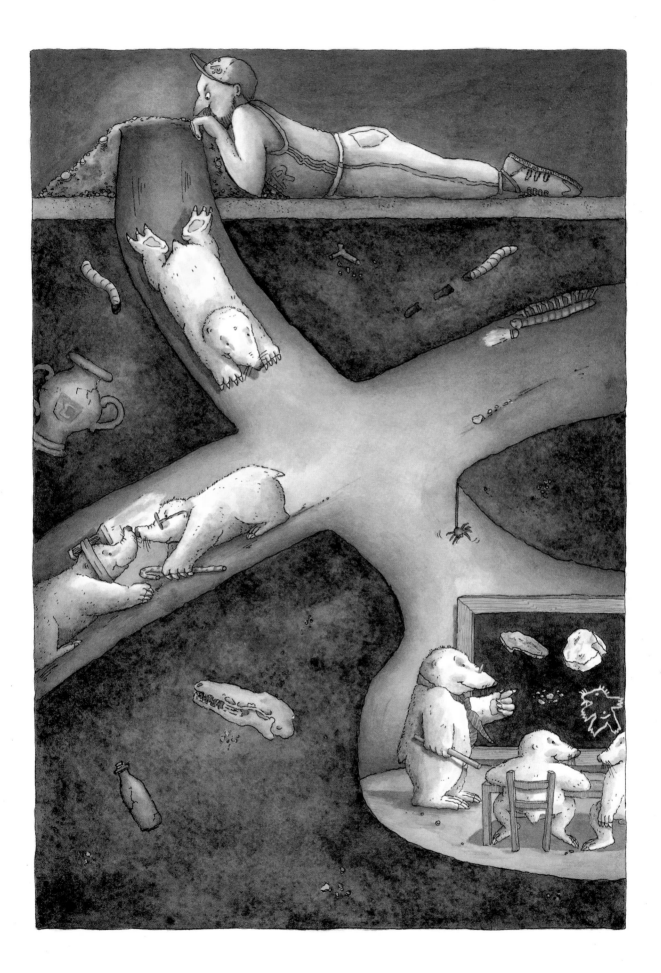

The next day, all anyone could talk about was
the strange mole who ate stone.

The mayor called together all the famous mole experts.
They measured the circumference of the mole's tunnel.
They studied its droppings:
they weighed them and smelled them and analyzed them . . .
Then they launched into a long experts' discussion,
which no one else understood at all.

Finally the experts went away, leaving the mayor
more confused than he was before they came.

This mole, however, was not alone.
Soon, our town was full of molehills.
We tripped over little hills of dirt and rubble everywhere.
And everywhere, the moles dug their tunnels:

under the sidewalks,
under the cathedral steps,
under the supermarket—
more precisely, next to checkout counter number 7 . . .

. . . and even under my bathtub!

That mole owes me his life.
Without me, he would have drowned in the bathwater.
I dried him off in my large fluffy towel
and offered him a small morsel of tile,
which he hungrily devoured.
He seemed very surprised
that a human being would be so kind to him.
Once he had regained his strength, he thanked me,
saying, "Peep peep peep!" then disappeared—
digging a small well-hidden hole behind the sink.

The situation grew worse and worse in our town.
The ground, which was now crisscrossed with tunnels,
would no longer support the weight of the buildings.

Houses leaned dangerously.
The streets became so full of holes and rubble
that no one was allowed to drive on them!

The mayor called an urgent meeting of the town council,
which voted unanimously to start a huge anti-mole campaign.
They put up posters everywhere, offering a reward
for all captured moles—dead or alive!

One morning, seven new fountains of water sprang up.
One of these spouted right in the middle of math class,
causing quite a diversion.
Still, if the moles were now attacking
the town's water pipes,
the situation was becoming urgent!

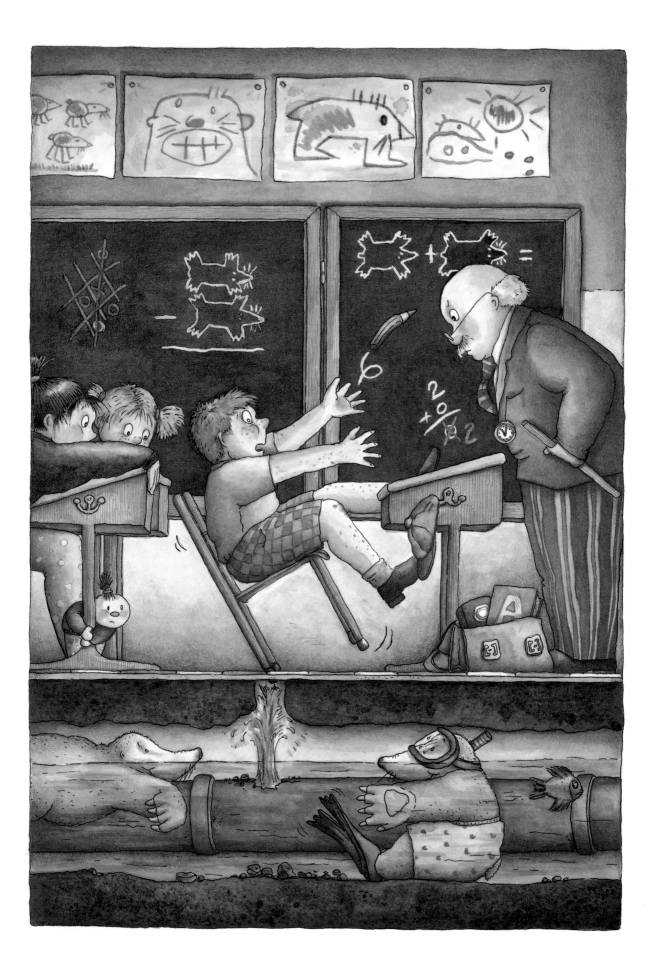

The next day when I got out of my bath, "my" mole
reappeared from the small hole that he had dug near the sink.
He first went over to my socks, sniffed them,
then said to me: "Peep peep."

"Peep peep," I responded and gave him a morsel of brick.
My mole squealed with pleasure and shook my hand
with his paw. Then he disappeared once again.

Outside, members of the anti-mole brigade took to the streets.
They patrolled the town armed with nets of steel
and long heavy clubs. They went after the stone moles without pity!
They meant to kill them! . . .

A few days later, my mole returned.

"Peep peep!" he said.

"Peep peep!" said a second mole who followed him.

A third, a fourth, and a fifth mole came out of the little hole.

At the sixth, I stopped counting.

The bathroom was soon overrun by dozens of little moles.

They began telling me their troubles,

all the while nibbling at my rock collection.

With tears in their eyes,

they told me about the cruelty of man.

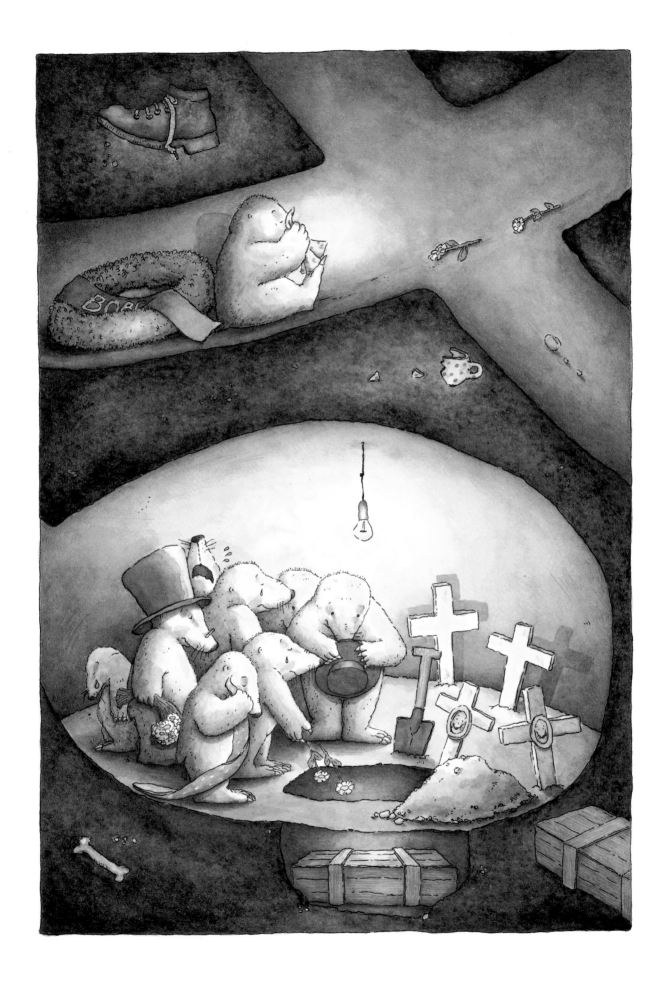

Some of them had lost their parents,
their brothers, their sisters, their friends . . .

Listening to them, I could feel my heart begin to tighten.
I tried to "peep" to the stone moles
that they had to understand man,
that the people of the town were afraid and angry.
No one likes to have a house come crashing down on them.
And it isn't funny for a worker who has just set his tiles
to have his work eaten before his very eyes.
The moles slowly nodded their heads.
They understood, and asked only that we find
a solution that would satisfy everyone.

So, I went to see the mayor.
I tried to explain to him that the moles were useful, peace-loving animals,
and that it was necessary to protect them, not to kill them . . .
But the mayor just got angry. "What about the unusable streets?
And the houses ready to collapse? And that!" he shouted,
pointing to a pile of rubble next to his desk.

Just then, a rock shattered one of the mayor's windows,
and we heard cries from the street below.
  "Down with stone moles! Down with stone moles!"
chanted the demonstrators.
I left the mayor's office, sad and discouraged.
What could I do, one voice against so many?

And then, I had an idea.
Why hadn't I thought of it before?

I returned to the mayor,
my idea hidden in my jacket pocket.
   "Look!" I said to the mayor.
   "Another mole!" he groaned, ready to get angry again.
   "Peep peep, pee-peep," I called out, and the mole turned around.
   "Now then, what would you like him to do?" I asked the mayor.
   "Well . . . make it jump on one leg," he said.
   "Peep, pee-peep peep," . . . and the mole hopped all around the office!
The mayor then demanded that the mole do
more and more difficult things.
And as soon as I "peeped" the order,
the mole did what the mayor asked.

Little by little, the mayor's face relaxed into a smile.

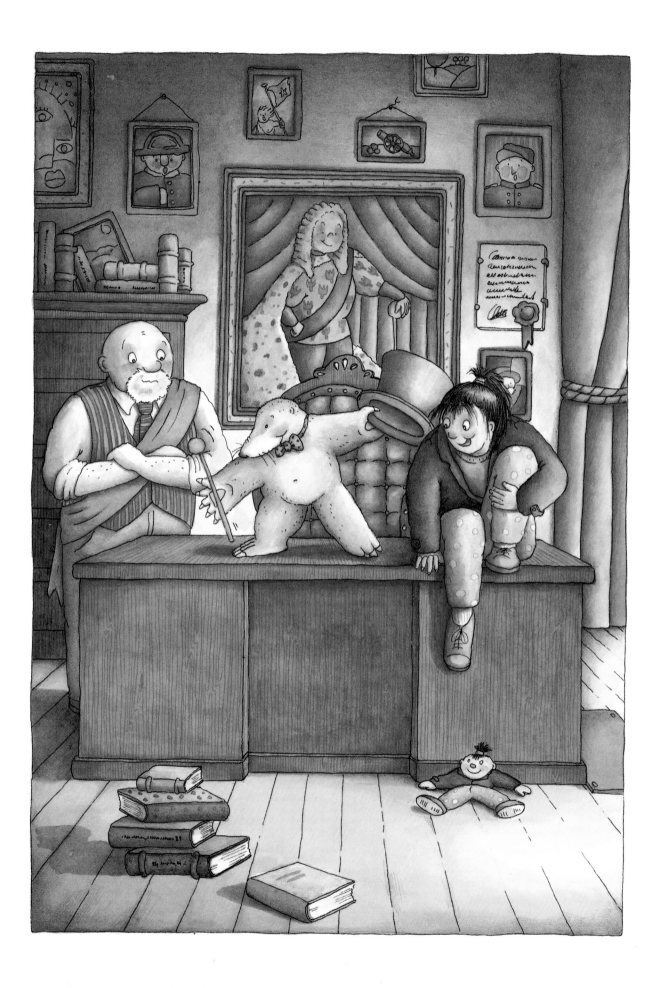

That very evening, all the townspeople gathered in the large town square
to hear an important announcement from the mayor.

"Men and moles must learn to become good friends," he declared.
The people did not believe their ears.

"Why should men tire themselves by doing all that dirty digging
in the ground," the mayor continued, "when our friends the stone moles
ask only to do it in our place?"

But not everyone was convinced.

"Peep pee-peeps," I called out finally.

One mole appeared, breaking through the pavement.

"Peep pee-peeps," I repeated.

And a second mole appeared, followed by a third, and a fourth . . .

Then, I showed everyone that the moles
would do just what I asked.

Today, in the middle of the town,
you can see an enormous rock.
This is where the stone moles now live.
And I am in charge of taking care of them.
If anyone has a nasty job to do,
like digging a cave or replacing telephone cables,
we come to the rescue.
Our town is always filled with visitors
who watch the comings and goings of "our" moles.
Everyone encourages them, everyone wishes them well,
and everyone admires their work.
Some people even bring them exotic stones from faraway countries—

ah, what a feast for the stone moles!

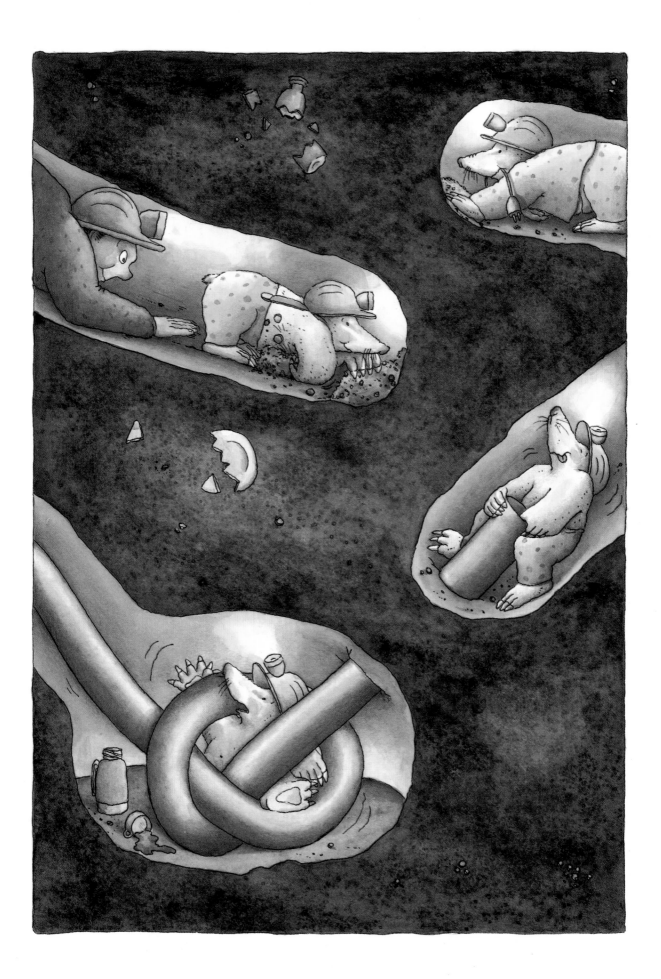